Turtle Spring

LILLIAN HOBAN

Greenwillow
Read-alone

GREENWILLOW BOOKS
A Division of William Morrow & Company, Inc., New York

Copyright © 1978 by Lillian Hoban. All rights reserved. No part of this book may
be reproduced or utilized in any form or by any means, electronic or mechanical, including
photocopying, recording or by any information storage and retrieval system,
without permission in writing from the Publisher. Inquiries should be addressed to
Greenwillow Books, 105 Madison Ave., New York, N.Y. 10016.
Printed in the United States of America.   First Edition
1 2 3 4 5 6 7 8 9 10

Library of Congress Cataloging in Publication Data
Hoban, Lillian.   Turtle spring.
(Greenwillow read-alone book) Summary: The Turtle family is puzzled by a very strange
bump under the lettuce bed in their garden. [1. Turtles—Fiction] I. Title.
PZ7.H635Tu [E] 77-15062 ISBN 0-688-80136-6 ISBN 0-688-84136-8 lib.bdg.

Dedicated to
the memory of
Chris Klotz—
who loved all things
in nature

One spring day Mrs. Turtle saw
a strange bump in her garden
right under the lettuce bed.

"Fred," she called to her husband.

"There's a very strange bump

in the garden

under the lettuce bed!"

Fred didn't answer.

He was busy spring-cleaning

his favorite rock.

"George," called Mrs. Turtle
to the oldest boy turtle.
"Run and tell your father
there is a very strange bump
under the lettuce bed!"

"Don't go near it, Ma," said George.

"It may be a bomb."

"Did you say

there is a bomb

under the bed, George?"

asked Lola,

the oldest girl turtle.

She dropped
her yo-yo
on the littlest
girl turtle's head.

"Sorry, Sis," she said.
"But there is a bomb under the bed
and we better run!"

"Run, run! There's a bomb
under the bed,"
yelled all the little turtle children.
They ran straight into
Mrs. Neighbor Turtle,
who had come to borrow a ribbon
for her new spring hat.

"I don't think much
of bombs under beds,"
said Mrs. Neighbor Turtle.
"Back home on our old pond
folks didn't mess
with such things."
And she went to tell her husband.

"Pa! Pa! Come quick!" yelled Sis.

"Our beds have bombs under them!"

"Is that a fact?" asked a robin

who had dropped in

for some spring gossip.

And he flew across the pond
to spread the news.
"Sis," said Mr. Turtle.
"That was very rude of you.
How many times
have I told you not to interrupt
when grown-ups are talking?"

"But, Pa," yelled all

the turtle children,

"there are bombs under the beds!"

"Now, children," said Mr. Turtle,
"I am busy spring-cleaning.
Go play somewhere else."

"Well," said George,

"if Pa won't listen,

we'll have to do it ourselves."

"Do what, George?

What should we do ourselves?"

cried all the other

little turtle children.

"Quiet," said George.
"I must sit down quietly
   and think what to do."
"Do! Do!" squawked a crow.
"It is spring and there is
   so much to do, do!"
"Quiet!" yelled George,
   and the crow flapped away.

Then George sat down quietly
by the edge of the pond.
All the other little turtle children
watched him think.

But it was not quiet.

PLIP PLIP PLIP

"This way, children,"

said Mrs. Green Snail,

popping out of the mud.

PLOP PLOP PLOP

A dozen baby snails

popped up after her.

"My, aren't they cute!"

said one

of the little

turtle children.

"Yes, and very bright

for their age, too,"

said Mrs. Snail.

"They are new

this spring.

Just born today!"

"QUIET!" yelled George.

"There's a bomb under the bed

and I can't think!"

"Drink! Drink! Drink!"

quacked Mrs. Duck

to her ducklings.

And she showed them

how to duck

head down, tail up,

in the pond.

PLINK PLINK PLINK

The little ducks

plunked into the water.

"Bottoms up! Bottoms up!"

quacked Mama Duck.

"That's lovely, my dears.
No one would think
you were just hatched
and new as the springtime!"

"QUIET!" roared George.

"There is a bomb under the bed,

and I must think.

Not another peep, do you hear?"

"PEEP PEEP PEEP!"

piped some spring peepers,

hopping into the pond.

"Peep hurray! Peep hurray!"

"What's all the fuss about?"
asked one of the little turtle children.

"It's springtime!" piped a peeper.

"Peep hurray! Peep hurray!
Peep hurray for spring!"

"Ssh!" said the little turtle children.
"There's a bomb under the bed
    and George can't think."
    But George was busy
    chasing a butterfly
    that was flitting and fluttering
    in the warm spring air.

"Well, if George won't do it,

I will," said Lola.

And she went off

into the woods to think.

The other little turtle children

followed her.

"George won't do it,

George won't do it!" they cried.

"Quiet," said Lola.

And she sat down

under a tree.

But it was not quiet.

"Chicka-dee-dee-doo!

A worm for you

and one for you

and one for you.

A seed for you

and one for you

and for you, too!

Open wide, my baby chicks,"

chirped Mrs. Chickadee.

"Open wide,

my chicka-dee-dee-dears!"

SWISH

SWISH

SWISH

A cloud of mayflies swarmed

in the spring air.

SHUSH

SHUSH

SHUSH

A little fuzzy caterpillar

crawled over a tender new leaf bud.

SSH SSH SSH

The catkins swayed

in the spring breeze.

"Be still, all of you!"
    yelled the little turtle children.
"There's a bomb under the bed,
    and Lola must think!"
    But Lola was busy picking
    bright new marsh marigolds
    in the warm spring sun.

"If Lola won't do it, I will,"
said Sis.
And she went off
into the garden to think.
All the other little turtle
children followed her, yelling,
"Lola won't do it!
Lola won't do it!"

"Quiet," said Sis Turtle.

And she sat down in the garden.

But it was not quiet.

There was

a very strange bump

in the garden

right under the lettuce bed.

It was eeping

and peeping

and chirping

and cheeping

and stirring

and heaving and

POW!

"Sis," whispered all the
turtle children quietly.
"The bomb is under the lettuce bed
and it is too late to think."

But Sis said, "Hush, hush.
It is spring, and I hear
the sweet sound
of new little turtles
on the land!"

And there,

coming out of the bump

right under the lettuce bed,

were ten little new little

dear little turtle children.

They were fresh out of their eggs,

and new as the spring,

and all peeping sweetly

in soft turtle voices.

"I knew I buried those eggs
  in the garden," said Mrs. Turtle.
"But I told them
  not to hatch till fall."

"Well, that's all right," said Mr. Turtle,

looking at his springtime babies.

"We can always make room for ten more."

And all the old little turtle children

thought so too.